THE WOMAN OF ANDROS

BY

THORNTON WILDER

MCMXXX — ALBERT & CHARLES BONI — NEW YORK

The first part of this novel is based upon the *Andria*, a comedy of Terence who in turn based his work upon two Greek plays, now lost to us, by Menander.

THE EARTH sighed as it turned in its course; the shadow of night crept gradually along the Mediterranean, and Asia was left in darkness. The great cliff that was one day to be called Gibraltar held for a long time a gleam of red and orange, while across from it the mountains of Atlas showed deep blue pockets in their shining sides. The caves that surround the Neapolitan gulf fell into a profounder shade, each giving forth from the darkness its chiming or its booming sound. Triumph had passed from Greece and wisdom from Egypt, but with the coming on of night they seemed to regain their lost honors, and the land that was soon to be called Holy prepared in the dark its wonderful burden. The sea was large enough to hold a varied weather: a storm played about Sicily and its smoking mountains, but at the mouth of the Nile the water lay like a wet pavement. A fair tripping breeze ruffled the Aegean and all the islands of Greece felt a new freshness at the close of day.

The happiest, and one of the least famous of the islands, Brynos, welcomed the breeze. The evening was long. For a time, the sound of the waves, briskly slapping against the wall of the little harbor, was covered by the chattering of women, by the shouts of boys, and by the crying of lambs. As the first lights appeared, the women retired; as the air was filled with the clangor of the shop fronts being put into place, the boys' voices ceased; and finally only the murmur of the men in the wineshops, playing at games with ivory counters, mingled with the sounds from the sea. A confused starlight, already apprehensive of the still unrisen moon, fell upon the tiers of small houses that covered the slope and upon the winding flights of stairs that served as streets between them.

The wineshops stood about the roughly paved square at the water's edge and in one of them the five or six principal fathers of the island sat playing. By the time the moon had risen, two of these, Simo and Chremes, had outstayed their companions. Simo was the owner of two warehouses; he was a trader and had three ships that passed continually to and fro among the islands. The men had finished playing; the counters lay on the table between them and they sighed into their beards as they thought of the long walk through the ghostly olive trees to their homes. Simo was more tired than usual: whereas the law of moderation teaches us that the mind cannot be employed for more than three hours daily over merchandise and numerals without soilure, he had that day spent five hours in argument and traffic.

"Simo," said Chremes suddenly, with the air of a man bracing himself to an unpleasant and long deferred task, "your boy is twenty-five now—"

Simo groaned as he saw the subject arising that he was never able to look in the face.

"It's four years," continued Chremes, "since you first said that a young man mustn't be forced into marriage by his old people. And certainly no one has been trying to force Pamphilus. But what is he waiting for? He helps you in the warehouse; he exercises in the field; he dines at the Andrian's. How many years must that kind of life go on before you agree with me that he would be better off married to my daughter?"

"Chremes, he must come to me of his own accord. I will not be the first one to speak about it to the boy."

"First! It won't be speaking of it first, Simo. It has been understood between our families for years that he will marry Philumena. It's being spoken of all the time. The young people tease him about it from morning to night. He knows perfectly well that my daughter is ready to marry him. It's sheer laziness on his part. It's sheer unwillingness to take on the responsibilities of being a husband and a father and the foremost young householder on the island."

"He's a young man who knows what he means to do. I will not coerce him."

"Then it's settled that he doesn't want

to marry my daughter. It's a humilia-
tion for her to be waiting all these years
for him to make up his mind, and her
mother's been after me to close the
matter for a long time. Perhaps I
shouldn't say it, but you'll be throwing
away a good thing through sheer hesi-
tancy, both of you. Philumena is by
far the healthiest and the prettiest girl
on any of these islands. And she's clever
at everything that is expected of a
woman in the home. The uniting of our
two families has advantages, Simo, that
I don't have to point out to you. But
this lapse of time has made it clear that
your son is going to wait until his fancy
has been caught by some other girl, I
suppose. So be it! From this very
night my wife is going to start looking
about for some other young man."

"Chremes, Chremes, he's only twenty-

five. Let him play about a little longer.
Why must they become husbands and
fathers so soon? He's good and he's
happy. So is your daughter. Let them
be awhile."

"Grandchildren!—that's what I want
to see. There shouldn't be a long step
between the generations. It's bad for
customs and manners."

"You'll make a greater mistake by
hurrying than by delaying."

"Well," Chremes continued, "there's
another reason why I want the matter
settled soon. And that is this: we don't
like the visits that Pamphilus is paying
to the Andrian woman. Naturally, Simo,
it's hard for me to be severe about it,
because my own son goes there too. But
it's natural that a father should be more
exacting in regard to his son-in-law than
in regard to his son."

Simo looked more uncomfortable than ever and remained silent. Chremes went on:

"I don't think you like this resort to foreign women any more than I do. Our islands have always been famous for strict and good behavior. If the devil was in us as boys we could always follow some shepherdess up a dark road. But this Andrian has brought the whole air of Alexandria to town with her, perfumes and hot baths and late hours."

Simo stroked his cheeks a moment and then replied in a low grunting voice: "Well, if it isn't one thing, it's another, I suppose. I don't know anything about this Andrian. The women seem to talk of nothing else from morning to night, but one can't believe what they say."

Thus invited, Chremes launched into his exposition with considerable relish, examining Simo's face from time to time to see if the details were arousing in him the interest they held for himself. "Her name is Chrysis, and I don't know what she means by calling herself Andrian. The island of Andros was never famous for such airs and graces as she puts on. She's flitted from Corinth and Alexandria, you may be sure. She should have stayed in her cities instead of burying herself in our town and reciting poetry to our young men. Yes, yes, she recites poetry to them like the famous ones. She has twelve or fifteen of them to dinner every seven or eight days,—the unmarried ones, of course. They lie about on couches and eat odd food and talk. Presently she rises and recites; she can recite whole tragedies without the book. She is very strict with the young men, apparently. She makes them

pronounce all the Attic accents; they
eat in the Athenian mode, drinking toasts
and wearing garlands, and each in turn
is elected King of the Banquet. And at
the close, hot towels are passed around
for them to wipe their hands on."

Simo did not concede to Chremes the
pleasure of his close interest; his eyes
were lowered and his face wore the same
bored expression that it brought to all
island gossip. Chremes decided to be
less expansive and added with easy indignation: "As for me, Alexandria is
Alexandria and Brynos is Brynos. A
few more imported notions and our island
will be spoiled forever. It will become a
mass of poor undigested imitations. All
the girls will be wanting to read and
write and declaim. What becomes of
home life, Simo, if women can read and
write? You and I married the finest

girls of our time and we've been happy. We can at least provide one more generation of good sense and good manners on this island before the age arrives when all the women will have the airs of dancers and all the men go about waiting on them."

Simo knew the answer to this, but he repressed it. Chremes, more than any man on the island, was ruled by his wife. In fact from her loom in the shadow, Chremes's wife tried to rule the whole island, using her harassed husband as her legislative and punitive arm. Simo asked:

"What happens after the banquet?"

"Each boy pays for his plate, and pays right smartly too, and from time to time one or another is graciously permitted to stay until morning. That's all I know."

"Is your son at all these dinners?"

"He was quarreling or something,— or perhaps he drank too much, I don't know. At all events, he was expelled for a time. Thrown right out into the street, he was, by the other guests. But he's made his peace with her again."

"Do you talk to him about this . . . this Chrysis?"

"Why, no. I pretend to know nothing about it."

"Is my son always there?"

"They say he's practically always there."

There was a long pause. The boy who attended in the wineshop went out into the moonlight and started putting up the shutters. Presently he returned and whispered to Simo that an old woman was waiting outside to speak to him and that she had been waiting there for some time. This was unusual on Brynos, but Simo took pride in never betraying any surprise. He nodded slightly and continued staring before him.

"Are there any other women at the Andrian's?" he asked.

"I don't know. Some say there are and some say there aren't. But there's a houseful of some sort. In fact it's a kind of hospital for the old and the lame and the . . . all kind of old battered pensioners. The house is way up at the edge of the town . . ."

"I know where it is."

". . . and the people, whoever they are, never come into town. They never even go out on the road by day. Oh, you can be sure the townspeople talk of nothing else."

Chremes rose and put on his cloak. He saw that Simo was as far as ever

from committing himself. "Well, that's
how it stands," he said. "I hope that in
another ten days you can give me a more
definite answer. My wife is after me a
good deal, Simo, and she says that I'm
to tell you this, that unless Pamphilus
stops those visits all idea of a marriage
between himself and Philumena is impossible. And that any such marriage
must be definitely settled pretty soon or
you'll have to start finding some other
girl one-tenth as good."

For the first time Simo bestirred himself and said slowly: "You and your
wife will be throwing away a good thing
too, Chremes. It's precisely because
Pamphilus is a great deal more than an
ordinary island boy that I can't speak
to him as I could to another son. There
are more sides to Pamphilus than you
imagine."

"Yes, Simo, we know that he's a fine young man. But we also know, if you will forgive me, that there's a strain in Pamphilus of the . . . the undecided, the procrastinating. To do his best and to take his place, Pamphilus must be urged on by someone, like yourself, whom he admires. And he's not as interested in this island and in what it stands for as he should be. Do you know the young priest of Æsculapius and Apollo? Well, there is something of the priest in Pamphilus. Such people aren't interested in putting their foot forward. They haven't yet come to see what life is about."

Chremes went out and plodded home along the rocky road. Simo sat on a minute longer. What a bad ending to a bad day, he thought. The two men had grown up on the island together. For thirty years they had been its leading citizens. They knew one another too well. In their conversation they had let play the faint antagonism that always lay between them. This boasting about their children,—how vulgar, how un-hellene. How unphilosophic. Yet that was true: there was something of the priest in Pamphilus.

❖   ❖   ❖

Simo turned to the old woman who was hiding in the shadow by the door. "You wanted to speak to me?" he asked roughly.

Between fright and suspense—for she had been waiting there for the greater part of two hours—Mysis was barely able to find her voice. "My mistress wishes to speak to you, sir,—Chrysis, the Andrian," and she pointed with both hands towards the waterfront.

Simo grunted. Looking up he saw the beautiful woman leaning against the parapet at the water's edge fifteen paces away. Her head and body were wrapped in veils, and she waited calmly and impersonally in the moonlight as though two hours were but a moment in her serenity. Below her in the little protected harbor the boats knocked against one another in friendly fashion, but all else was still under the melancholy and peace of the moon. Simo approached her without deference and said: "Well?"

"I am—" she began.

"I know who you are."

She paused and began again. "I am in an extremity. I am driven to ask a service of you." Simo pushed his lips forward, raised his eyebrows, and lowered his eyes wearily. She continued in an even voice without anxiety or suppliance: "A friend of mine is very ill on the island of Andros from which I come. Twice I have sent this friend money by the hands of various sea-captains going between the islands. I know now that the captains are dishonest and that my money never reaches him. All that I ask is that you put your frank upon the package of money and it will reach him."

Simo did not like to see women carrying themselves, as this Andrian did, with dignity and independence. His antagonism was increased; he asked abruptly: "Who is this friend?"

"He was formerly a sea-captain," she replied, still without servility. "But now he is not only ill; he is insane. He is

insane by reason of the hardships he endured in the war. I have put him in
charge of some people, but they will
only be kind to him as long as I send
them money for it. Otherwise they will
put him away on a small island nearby
with the others. You know such islands
... where basins of food are left for
them every few days ... and where—"

"Well," said Simo harshly, "since your
friend has lost the use of his reason and
since he cannot realize the conditions
under which he lives, it is best that you
leave him upon the island with the others.
Is that not so?"

Chrysis tightened her lips and looked
far out over his head. "I have no answer
for that," she replied. "It may be true
for you, but it is not true for me. This
man was once a very famous sea-captain.
You may have known him. His name

was Philocles. Now I think I am his only friend, unless you choose to help him also."

Simo did not acknowledge having known him, but the tone in his next words was less vindictive. "When would you like this money to go?"

"I . . . I have some money ready now, but I would prefer to send some in ten days."

"What is your name?"

"My name is Chrysis, daughter of Arches of Andros."

"Chrysis, I will do this for you, and I will even add to the sum. In return you will do a favor for me. You will refuse my son entrance into your house."

Chrysis moved slightly to one side and stretching her arm along the parapet looked down into the harbor. "Favors cease to be favors when there are conditions attached to them, Simo. Magnanimity does not bargain with its powers." These maxims were almost murmured; then she raised her head and said to him: "I cannot do that, unless I tell your son that it is because you have ordered it."

Simo's slightly cynical superiority over the rest of the world reposed on the fact that he had gone through life without ever having been surprised as unjust, untruthful, or ungenerous. Angry, but with himself, for having been caught at this disadvantage, he replied: "That is not necessary. It would be quite simple for your servant to tell him that you do not wish him to come into the house."

"I could not do that. There are several young men on the island to whom my door, for one reason or another, is closed.

I cannot do that to Pamphilus without
giving him a reason. If you understood
the spirit of our group you would not wish
me to do that; I think that there we
are not lacking in respect for one another.
I hardly know your son; I have scarcely
exchanged twenty words with him; but
I know that he is by far the first young
man among my guests." Suddenly the
image of Pamphilus rose up before her
and she was filled with an excitement and
joy in praising him, and for that very
reason she subdued herself and added in
a lower voice: "He is old enough to make
decisions for himself. And if I do this,
he must understand."

Simo was aware that some strange wise
praise of his son hovered between them
and his heart almost stopped beating for
pleasure, but from his lips there rushed
the brutal phrase he had prepared a

moment before: "Then you must send your money to Andros some other way."

"Very well," she said.

They stood looking at one another. Simo suddenly realized that he lived among people of thin natures and that he was lonely; he was out of practice in conversing with sovereign personalities whose every speech arose from resources of judgment and inner poise. With his wife, with Chremes, with the islanders one could talk with half one's mind and still hold one's authority, but here in a few moments this woman had caught him twice at a disadvantage. Chrysis saw this and came to his aid; she broke the silence that was leaving him obstinate, angry, and small.

"It is perhaps his younger brother whose life can be arranged for him; your Pamphilus deserves to be better under-

stood than that." And her tone im-
plied: "You and he are of one measure
and should stand on the same side."

Simo preferred talking about his sons
to any other activity in the world, but
his emotions were very mixed as he as-
sembled an answer to this remark:

"Well, well . . . Andrian, I will frank
your money for you. I have boats going
to Andros every twelve days. One went
off today."

"I thank you."

"Could I ask you . . .euh . . . not to
mention this to Pamphilus?"

"I shall not."

"Well . . . well, good night."

"Good night."

Simo trudged home in an unaccustomed
elation. It made him happy to hear
Pamphilus praised and "probably this
woman was an exceptional judge of

persons." He had made a fool of himself, but in good hands one does not mind. "Life . . . life . . .," he said to himself, hunting for a generalization that would describe its diversity, its power of casting up from time to time on the waves of tedious circumstance such starlike persons. The generalization did not arrive, but he walked on in a bright astonishment. How he would like to hear her read a play; he used to be interested in such things and when his journeys took him to an island that was large enough to have a theatre he never missed an opportunity to hear a good tragedy.

As he entered the courtyard of his farm he saw Pamphilus standing alone, looking at the moon.

"Good evening, Pamphilus," he said.

"Good evening, father."

Simo went to bed, deeply moved with pride, but for form's sake he repeated anxiously to himself: "I don't know what I'll do with him. I don't know what I'll do with him."

And Pamphilus stood looking at the moon and thinking about his father and mother. He was thinking about them in the light of a story that Chrysis had told. As the banquets drew to a close she liked to move the conversation away from local comment and to introduce some debate upon an abstract principle. (She cited often the saying of Plato that the true philosophers are the young men of their age. "Not," she would add, "because they do it very well; but because they rush upon ideas with their whole soul. Later one philosophizes for praise, or for apology, or because it is a complicated intellectual game.") Pamphilus remembered that on one evening the conversation had turned upon the wrong that poets do in pretending that life is heroic. And a boy from the other end of the island had said, half-mockingly and half-hopefully: "Well, you know, Chrysis . . . you know, life in a family is not in the same world as life in Euripides."

Chrysis sat a moment searching for her answer, then she lifted her hand and said: "Once upon a time—"

The table burst out laughing, but with an affectionate laugh of mock-repudiation, because they knew that she liked to cast her remarks into the form of fables and to begin them with this childish formula. Pamphilus heard again her beautiful voice saying:

"Once upon a time there was a hero who had done a great service to Zeus. When he came to die and was wandering

in the gray marshes of Hell, he called to
Zeus reminding him of that service and
asking a service in return: he asked to
return to earth for one day. Zeus was
greatly troubled and said that it was not
in his power to grant this, since even he
could not bring above ground the dead
who had descended to his brother's king-
dom. But Zeus was so moved by the
memory of the past that he went to the
palace of his brother and clasping his
knees asked him to accord him this favor.
And the King of the Dead was greatly
troubled, saying that even he who was
King of the Dead could not grant this
thing without involving the return to life
in some difficult and painful condition.
But the hero gladly accepted whatever
difficult or painful condition was involved, and the King of the Dead permitted him to return not only to the

earth, but to the past, and to live over
again that day in all the twenty-two
thousand days of his lifetime that had
been least eventful; but that it must be
with a mind divided into two persons,—
the participant and the onlooker: the
participant who does the deeds and says
the words of so many years before, and
the onlooker who foresees the end. So
the hero returned to the sunlight and to
a certain day in his fifteenth year.

"My friends," continued Chrysis, turning her eyes slowly from face to face, "as
he awoke in his boyhood's room, pain
filled his heart,—not only because it had
started beating again, but because he
saw the walls of his home and knew that
in a moment he would see his parents
who lay long since in the earth of that
country. He descended into the courtyard. His mother lifted her eyes from

the loom and greeted him and went on with her work. His father passed through the court unseeing, for on that day his mind had been full of care. Suddenly the hero saw that the living too are dead and that we can only be said to be alive in those moments when our hearts are conscious of our treasure; for our hearts are not strong enough to love every moment. And not an hour had gone by before the hero who was both watching life and living it called on Zeus to release him from so terrible a dream. The gods heard him, but before he left he fell upon the ground and kissed the soil of the world that is too dear to be realized."

It was with such eyes that Pamphilus now saw his father pass into the house and that he had seen his mother moving about, covering the fire and going about the last tasks of the day. And it was in the light of that story that his eyes had been opened to the secret life of his parents' minds. It seemed suddenly as though he saw behind the contentment and the daily talkativeness into the life of their hearts—empty, resigned, pathetic and enduring. It was Chrysis's reiterated theory of life that all human beings— save a few mysterious exceptions who seemed to be in possession of some secret from the gods—merely endured the slow misery of existence, hiding as best they could their consternation that life had no wonderful surprises after all and that its most difficult burden was the incommunicability of love. Certainly that explained the humorous sadness of his father and the fretful affection of his mother. And now as his father passed him in the courtyard this interpretation shook him more forcibly than ever.

What can one do for them? What—to be equal to them—can one do for oneself? He was twenty-five already, that is—no longer a young man. He would soon be a husband and a father, a condition he did not invest with any glamour. He would soon be the head of this household and this farm. He would soon be old. Time would have flowed by him like a sigh, with no plan made, no rules set, no strategy devised that would have taught him how to save these others and himself from the creeping gray, from the too-easily accepted frustration.

"How does one live?" he asked the bright sky. "What does one do first?"

❖   ❖   ❖

Chrysis's view of human experience expressed itself, as we have seen, in fables, in quotations from literature, in proverbs and in mottoes. Herself she summed up in a word: she regarded herself as having "died." Dead then as she was, the inconveniences of her profession, the sneers of the villagers, the ingratitude of her dependents, no longer had the power to disturb her. The only thing that troubled her in her grave was the recurrence, even in her professional associations, of a wild tenderness for this or that passerby, brief and humiliating approaches to love. These experiences and any others that were able to depress her, she now dismissed as weakness, as pride, as an old, rebellious and unwhipped vanity. The morning after the conversation with Simo at the water's edge she awoke strangely troubled; but she resolved not to exam-

ine the new dejection. It floated all day
above her head,—a voice repeating: "I
am alone. Why have I never seen that
before? I am alone." Indeed the profession she followed was one of those that
emphasize the dim notion that lies at the
back of many minds: the notion that we
are not necessary to anyone, that attach-
ments weave and unweave at the mercy
of separation, satiety and experience.
The loneliest associations are those that
pretend to intimacy.

But she had discovered two ways of
mitigating this unresponsiveness and in-
stability in the world she lived in. The
first was the development she brought to
the institution of the hetaira's banquet.
She took endless pains over these re-
unions and to the wide-eyed guests they
seemed indeed all that one could conceive
of wit and eloquence and aristocratic

ease. Great talkers are so constituted
that they do not know their own thoughts
until, on the tide of their particular gift,
they hear them issuing from their mouths.
Chrysis gave herself that luxury, the
luxury of talking to these young men
from her whole mind. Much of it lay
beyond their reach; but her refusal to
condescend, her assumption that the
analysis of ideas and of masterpieces was
their natural element, excited them. She
knew that apart from her beauty she
was not particularly fitted for her calling; she lacked the high spirits that please
the customers of middle age; but younger
men, who still approach love with a
touch of awe, are not so disappointed
with those common exercises when they
find them invested with melancholy,
dignity and literature. Perhaps the ma-
turity of a civilization can be judged by

this trait, by observing whether the young
men first fall in love with women older or
younger than themselves; if in their
youth their imaginations pass their time
in hallowing the images of prattling un-
nourishing girls their natures will be
forever after the thinner. But even at
their best Chrysis's guests seemed remote and immature to her and finally
she discovered a second way of making
life more stable and her friends more
constant: she adopted stray human
beings that needed her.

In the inner monologue of her thoughts
Chrysis called these dependents her
"sheep." And although they were
gathered into her shelter from places
and moments of fearful extremity, they
became accustomed to their new comfort
with extraordinary rapidity. In fact
their past trials began to take on a ro-

mantic color and when anything in the
present situation did not suit them they
had been known to regret the lost felicities of the slave-markets, the mills and
the massacred villages. For Chrysis
human nature no longer had many surprises and the manner in which the sheep
scolded and even condescended to their
shepherd did not deject her. She loved
them and was sufficiently repaid by occa-
sional hours of a late afternoon when the
odd group would sit in the garden, weaving in amity and humor. Such hours almost resembled life in a home.

There was to be a banquet that evening,
so shaking her head at the shadow that
hovered above her she descended into the
town to do the marketing. She was accompanied by Mysis and the porter,—
Mysis carrying a net to hold the fruit
and the salad-greens, and the porter a

large jar to be filled with salt-water and
then with fish and shell-fish. Chrysis
moved slowly down the long twisting
flights of stairs. She was wrapped about
by a great scarf of antique finely-wrinkled
material and wore a broad-brimmed Tan-
agran hat of woven straw. The one hand
that appeared outside the folds of her
scarf carried a small wooden fan. It was
her business to be invested with the re-
moteness and glamour of a legend, for at
that time Greek taste turned upon a
nostalgia for the antique; it was her
business to be as different from other
women as possible and to convert that
difference into money. The shops and
temporary booths were all on the open
square at the water's edge and there in
the bright sunlight the most excitable
and loquacious of races was enjoying its
morning tumult; but as this calm and

day-dreaming figure appeared above them
a hush fell upon the bargainers. This
was the very deportment the Greek
women lacked and sighed for. They were
short and swarthy and shrill, and their
incessant conversation was accompanied
by the incessant play of their hands. The
whole race was haunted by a passionate
admiration for poise and serenity and
slow motion, and now for an hour the
Andrian's every move was followed by
the furtive glances of the islanders, with
mingled awe and hatred. The Brynians,
when she appeared, felt themselves to be
provincial and commercial. From time
to time some of the young men who had
been guests at her house approached her
and spoke to her. Then it was that the
unmarried girls and the young wives of
the island gazed with consternation and
fallen jaw at the way she smiled and

talked and dismissed their brothers and
their future husbands. Philumena, in
the shadow of an awning, leaned back
against a wall and watched the stranger;
turning her head slightly she could see
Pamphilus at the tally-desk in the door
of his father's warehouse. Her eyes fell
on her rough gown and her red arms and
a long slow blush mounted to her face.
But all the while Chrysis's heart had
been growing heavier. "I have lived
alone and I shall die alone," it said, and
groaned within her.

As she returned to her house from the
market she fell into a feverish monologue.
"The fault is in me. It's my lack of
perseverance in affection. I know that.
Now, Chrysis, you must begin your life
over again; you must assemble some
plan. You must devote yourself with all
your mind to your sheep. You must

break down all their coldness and wilfulness. You must make yourself love them again. You must bring back the happiness you felt with each one of them when you first knew them. It is routine, it is the daily contact that has spoiled all that. It's cowardly of me to be able to love people only when they are new. Now, now, Chrysis!—arise!" For the hundredth time she was visited by hope and courage. She would win in this thing. As she approached the house she was all but stumbling in her eagerness; she would create a home. "If I love them enough, I can understand them," she muttered. "One never learns how to live, or one's lights on living arrive too late, when one has spoiled the surrounding situation, spoiled it beyond repair. But I am to be on the earth for fifty years, and I must do it."

THE WOMAN

Chrysis did not realize what took place in the house during her absences, and that when she left it the house was empty. The personalities of her flock were extinguished. They fretted; they hovered about the gates peering in the direction from which she would return, and their minds ceased to act save in terms of that resentment which is the complement of devotion. She did not realize that this wasting of love in fretfulness was one of the principal activities on the planet. When she was away fear descended upon them; their dependence upon her was so great that even her temporary absences reminded them of the destitution from which they had been lifted,—circumstances so fearful that their conscious minds never revisited them, but which hovered in the distance enriching their present ease and hardening their self-centredness. All this antagonism therefore met her in a flood as she stumbled across the threshhold of her home. By the middle of the afternoon she was saying to herself, almost in a panic: "It is impossible. I can do nothing. They even hate me. But fortunately I am dead. It is not my pride that is hurt. I am at peace in the ground. Yet oh! if only we had some help in these matters. If only the gods were sometimes present among us. To have nothing to go by except this idea, this vague idea, that there lies the principle of living!"

During the banquet she looked about her for comfort. "It is also cowardly of me to be happy only at the banquets where I can lead the conversation and display my thoughts and be admired." But tonight even that exhilaration was wanting; her guests seemed younger and remoter than ever, and she in turn was capricious and all but irritable. It was to be expected, therefore, that the conversation would take turns little likely to comfort her.

Niceratus, one of the more assured of her guests, asked her what life would be like in two thousand years.

"Why," she said at once, "there will be no more war."

"I should not wish to be alive in a world where there was no war," he replied. "That would be an age of women."

Now Chrysis was jealous of the dignity of women and lost no occasions to combat such hasty disparagements. She leaned forward and asked encouragingly:

"You wish to serve the state, Niceratus?"

"I do."

"And you admire courage?"

"I do, Chrysis."

"Then go bear children," she replied, turning away.

Niceratus found this remark unseemly and left the house. (He absented himself from the two successive banquets, but later returned and asked her pardon for making a personal grievance out of a difference of opinion. Confessions of error always gave Chrysis great pleasure. "Happy are the associations," she would say, "that have grown out of a fault and a forgiveness.")

The conversation then turned upon the plays concerning Medea and Phaedra which she had read to them at an earlier banquet and upon all manifestations of extravagant passion. The young men declared that the problem was not as complicated as it appeared to be and that such women should have been whipped like disobedient slaves and shut up in a room with a jar of water and a little plain food until their pride was subdued. They then recounted to her, almost in whispers, the story of a girl from a village on the further side of the island whose behavior had thrown her family and her friends into consternation. The girl had continued for a time, glorying in her disorders, until one morning, rising early, she had climbed a high cliff near her home and thrown herself into the sea. A silence fell on the company as all turned inquiringly to Chrysis asking for the explanation of such a reversal.

To herself she said: "Do not try to explain to them. Talk of other things. Stupidity is everywhere and invincible." But their continued expectancy prevailed upon her. She seemed to struggle with herself for a moment, deeply troubled, and then began in a low voice: "Once upon a time the great army of women came together to a meeting. And they invited to this meeting one man, a tragic poet. They told him that they wished to send a message to the world of men and that he was to be their advocate and mouthpiece. 'Tell them,' said the women eagerly, 'that it is only in appearance that we are unstable. Tell them that this is because we are hard-pressed and in bitter servitude to nature, but that at heart, only asking their patience, we are as steadfast, as brave and as manly as they.' The poet smiled sadly, saying that the men who knew this already would merely be ashamed to be told it again, and the men who did not know it would learn nothing through the mere telling; but he consented to deliver the message. The men at first were silent, then one by one they broke out into laughter. And they sent the poet back to the army of women with these words: 'Tell them not to be anxious and not to trouble their pretty heads with these matters. Tell them that their popularity is not dying out, and let them not endanger it through heroics.' When the poet had repeated these words to the women, some blushed with shame and some with anger; some rose with a weary sigh: 'We should never have spoken to them,' they said. They went back to their mirrors and started combing their hair and as they combed their hair they wept."

Chrysis had barely finished this story when a young man who had hitherto taken little part in the conversation suddenly launched into a violent condemnation of her means of livelihood. This youth was of that temper that seeks to mould the lives of others abruptly to certain patterns of its own choosing. He now commanded Chrysis to become a servant or a sempstress. The other guests began to whisper among themselves and to avert their faces from confusion and anger, but Chrysis sat gazing at his flashing eyes and admiring his earnestness. There was a certain luxury in having an external mortification added to an inner despair. She was already troubled by her recent discomfiture of Niceratus and now chose to be magnanimous. She arose and approached the young fanatic; taking his hand she smiled at him with grave affection, saying to the company: "It is true that of all forms of genius, goodness has the longest awkward age."

But these incidents were not of a nature to distract her mind from the protracted oppression of the day. "Vain. Empty. Transitory," the voice within her repeated. But just as she was about to finish the day with the comprehensive summary that she had nothing to lend to life and no place to fill, her eyes fell upon Pamphilus. It was his custom, through lack of self-confidence, to take the last seat at the remote end of the room. The guests acknowledged his preëminence among them, but when one evening they had wished to elect him King of the Banquet he had furtively and savagely intimated to them his refusal and the votes had passed to another. But Chrysis's eyes had often, as now, rested upon that head bent forward to receive her every word and that received each one with so earnest a frown.

"That is something!" she said to herself suddenly and for a moment her heart stopped beating.

She had intended to recite to them *The Clouds* of Aristophanes that evening, but she now changed her mind. She felt the need to nourish her heart and those watchful eyes with something lofty and deeply felt. Perhaps what she called the "lofty" was in this world merely a beautiful form of falsehood, cheating the heart. But she would try again tonight and see whether, after so dejected a day, it woke any stir of conviction. "What shall I read?" she asked herself as the tables were being removed. "Something from Homer?—Priam begging of Achilles the body of Hector? No. . . . No. . . . Nor would they understand the *Oedipus at Colonus*. The *Alcestis?* The *Alcestis?*"

One of the shyer guests, seeing her de-

liberating over the choice of the evening's
declamation, timidly asked her to read
the *Phaedrus* of Plato.

"Oh, my friend," she said, "I have not
seen the book for several years. I should
be obliged to improvise long stretches in
it. . . ."

"Could you . . . could you read the
opening and the close?"

"I shall try it for you," she replied and
rising slowly disposed the folds of her
robe about her. The servants withdrew
and silence fell upon the company. This
was the moment (on happier evenings)
that she loved; this hush, this eagerness,
this faintly mocking affection. What
drives them—she would ask herself—in
the next fifteen years to become so grace-
less . . . so pompous, or envious, or so
busily cheerful?

At first all went well. The boys

listened with delight to the account of how other young men gathered in the streets and palaestra of Athens to hear the arguments of Socrates. Listening, they agreed that nothing in the world was more to be prized than a beautifully ordered speech. Then followed the description of the walk that Socrates and Phaedrus took into the country. *"This is indeed a rare resting-place. This plane-tree is not only tall, but thick and spreading. And this agnus castus is at the very moment of flowering and its shade and its fragrance will render our stay the more agreeable. These images and these votive-offerings tell us that the place is surely sacred to some nymphs and to some river-god. . . . Truly, Phaedrus, you are an admirable guide."*

From there she passed to the close:

"But let us go now, as the heat of the day is over.

"*Socrates: Would it not be well before we go to offer up a prayer to the gods of this place?*

"*Phraedus: It would, Socrates.*

"*Socrates: Beloved Pan, and all ye other gods who haunt this place, grant that I may become beautiful in the inner man and may whatever I possess without be in harmony with that which is within. May I esteem the wise men alone to be rich. And may my store of gold be such as none but the good may bear. Phaedrus, need we say anything more? As for myself I have prayed enough.*

"*Phaedrus: And let the same prayer serve for me, for these are the things friends share with one another.*"

All went well until this phrase. Then Chrysis, the serene, the happily dead, seeing the tears that stood in the eyes of Pamphilus, could go no further, and before

them all she wept as one weeps who after
an absence of folly and self-will returns
to a well-loved place and an old loyalty.
It was true, true beyond a doubt, tragi-
cally true, that the world of love and
virtue and wisdom was the true world
and her failure in it all the more overwhelming. But she was not alone; he
too saw the long and failing war as she
did, and she loved him as though she
were loving for the first time and as one
is never able to love again. That was
sealed; that was forever assigned.

After a few moments she collected herself and quieted the guests who had risen
in concern about her. "Sit down, my
friends. I am ready now," she said
smiling. "I shall read you *The Clouds* of
Aristophanes."

But it was some time before the
laughter rose among the couches, the

laughter that was a just tribute to the divine wit of the poet of *The Clouds*.

❖ ❖ ❖

Brynos rose with the dawn, and it was not many hours later that the morning's work was over. Several days after the conversation recorded above, Pamphilus, having helped his father in the warehouse and being in no mood for exercising in the field, started out to walk to the highest point on the island. It was early Spring. A strong wind had blown every cloud from the sky and the sea lay covered with flying white-tipped waves. His garments leapt and billowed about him and his very hair tugged at his head. The gulls themselves, leaning upon the gusts,

were caught unawares from time to time
and blown with ruffled feathers and scan-
dalized cries towards the violet-blue
zenith. Pamphilus led his life with much
worry and self-examination and all the
exhilaration of wind and sun could not
drive from his mind the anxious affection
with which he now turned over his
thoughts of Chrysis and Philumena and
of the four members of his family. He
was straying among the rocks and the
lizards and the neglected dwarfed olive-
trees, when his attention was suddenly
caught by an incident on the hillside to
his left. A group of boys from the town
was engaged in tormenting a young girl.
She was retreating backwards up the
slope through a disused orchard, shout-
ing haughtily back at her pursuers. The
boys' malice had turned to anger; they
were retorting hotly and letting fly about

her a few harmless stones. Pamphilus strode over to the group and with a gesture ordered the boys down the hill. The girl, her face still flushed and distrustful, stood with her back against a tree and waited for him to come towards her. They looked at one another for a moment in silence. Finally Pamphilus said:

"What is the matter?"

"They're just country fools, that's all. They've never seen anyone before who didn't come from their wretched Brynos." And then from rage and disappointment she began to cry uncontrollably and despairingly.

Pamphilus watched her for a time and then asked her where she had been going.

"Nowhere. I was just going for a walk and they followed me from the town. I can't do anything. I can't go anywhere. . . . I wasn't hurting them. I was just going for a walk alone and they called names after me. They followed me way up here; I called names at them and then they started throwing things at me. That's all."

"I thought I knew everyone on the island," said Pamphilus thoughtfully, "but I have never seen you before. Have you been here long?"

"Yes, I've been here almost a year," she replied, adding indistinctly, ". . . but I hardly ever go out or anything."

"You hardly ever go out?"

"No," and she fumbled with her dress and stared at the sea, frowning.

"You should try to know some of the other girls and go out for walks with them."

This time she turned and looked into his face. "I don't know any of the other

girls. I . . . I live at home and they
don't let me go out of the house, except
when I go out for walks nights with . . .
well, with Mysis." She continued to be
shaken with sobs, but she was adjusting
her hair and the folds of her dress. "I
don't see why they have to throw stones
at me," she added.

Pamphilus looked at her in silence,
gravely. Presently he collected himself
and said: "There's a big smooth stone
over there. Will you go over there and
sit down?"

She followed him to the stone, still
busy with her hair and drawing her
fingers across her eyes and cheeks.

"I have a sister just about your age,"
said Pamphilus. "You can begin by
knowing her. You can go for walks with
her and then you wouldn't be a stranger
any more. Her name is Argo. You'd

like one another, I know. My sister is weaving a large mantle for my mother and she'd like you to help her with it and she could help you with yours. Are you making a mantle?"

"Yes."

"That would be fine," said Pamphilus, and from that moment Glycerium loved him forever.

"I probably know your father, don't I?" he asked.

"I have no father," she replied, looking up at him weakly, "I am the sister of the woman from Andros."

"Oh . . . oh . . .," said Pamphilus, more astonished than he had ever been in his life. "I know your sister well."

"Yes," said Glycerium. Her bright wet eyes strayed over the streaked sea and the blown birds. "She doesn't want anyone to know that I'm there. All day

I stay up on the top of the house or work
in the court. Only at night I'm allowed
to go for a walk with Mysis. Even now
I'm supposed to be in the house, but I
broke my promise. She has gone to the
market and so I broke my promise. I
wanted to see what the island and the
sea look like by day. And I wanted to
look across to Andros where I come from.
But the boys followed me here and threw
stones at me and I can never come
again."

Here she fell to weeping even more despairingly than before and Pamphilus
could do nothing but say "Well" several
times and "Yes." At last he asked her
what her name was.

"Glycerium. Chrysis went away from
home a long time ago and I was living
with my brother and he died and I
couldn't live with him any more. And

I had nowhere to go or anything, and one day she came back and took me to live with her. That's all."

"Have you any brothers or sisters?"

"Oh, no."

"Who is Mysis?"

"Mysis isn't Greek. She is from Alexandria. Chrysis found her. All of them in the house,—she just found them somewhere. That's what she does. Mysis was a slave in the cloth mills. Sometimes she tells me about it."

Pamphilus still gazed at her, and bringing back her wandering evasive glance from the sea she looked at him from her thin face and enormous hungry eyes. Even a long glance did not now embarrass them.

"Do you want me to ask Chrysis to let you go about the island by day?" he asked.

"If she doesn't want it, we mustn't

change her. Chrysis knows best." She turned away from him and said in a lower voice, dreamy and embittered: "But what can become of me? Am I always to stay locked up? I am fifteen already. The world is full of wonderful things and people that I might never know about. I know it was wrong of me to break my promise; but to live for years without ever knowing new people,—to hear them passing the door all day, and to see them a long ways off. Do you think I did very wrong?"

"No."

"I don't know anyone. I don't know anyone."

"Well . . . well, you'll come to know my sister. That will be a beginning," he said, taking her fingertips thoughtfully and wonderingly in his.

"Yes," she said.

"Everything is beginning over again. I'm your friend. Then my sister. Soon you will have a great many. You'll see."

"But where will I be five years from now and ten years from now," she cried, staring about her wildly. "I don't know. I'm afraid. I'm unhappy. Everyone in the world is happy except me."

The caress of the hands in first love, and never so simply again, seems to be a sharing of courage, an alliance of two courages against a confusing world. As his hand passed from her hair to her shoulder, she turned to him with·parted lips and hesitant eyes, then suddenly bound both her arms about his neck. Into his ears her lips wildly and all but meaninglessly repeated: "Yes. Yes. Yes. I can't stay there forever. I should never know anyone. I should never see anybody."

"She will let you come to see me," he said.

"No," said Glycerium. "But I'll come by myself. I mustn't ask her. She would not let me come. She always knows best. And the boys can throw their stones. I don't mind if you're here. What . . . what is your name?"

"My name is Pamphilus, Glycerium."

"Can . . . can I call you by it?"

It was not at this meeting, nor at their next, but at the third, beneath the dwarfed olive-trees, that those caresses that seemed to be for courage, for pity and for admiration, were turned by Nature to her own uses.

These conversations took place in the early Spring. One afternoon in the late Summer Chrysis slipped out of her house and climbed the hill behind it. She was filled with a great desire to be alone and to think. She looked out over the glittering sea. The winds were moderate on that afternoon and before them the innumerable neat waves hurried towards the shore, running up the sands with a long whisper, or discreetly lifting against the rocks a scarf of foam. In the distance a school of dolphins engaged at their eternal games led the long procession of curving backs. The water was marbled at intervals with the strange fields and roadways of a lighter blue; and behind all she beheld with love the violet profile of Andros. For a time she strayed about upon the crest of the hill, making sure that no one was watching or following her, then descending the further side she sought out her favorite retreats, a point of rock that projected into the sea and a sheltered cove beside it. As she drew near the place, she stumbled forward, almost running, and as she went she murmured soothingly to herself: "We are almost there. Look, we are almost there now." At last, climbing over the boulders she let herself down into an amphitheatre of hot dry sand. She started unbinding her hair, but stopped herself abruptly: "No, no. I must think. I should fall asleep here. I must think first. I shall come back soon," she muttered to the amphitheatre, and continuing her journey she reached the furthermost heap of stones and sat down. She rested her chin upon her hand and fixing her eyes upon the horizon she waited for the thoughts to come.

The first thing to think about was her new illness. Several times she had been awakened by a wild fluttering in her left side that continued, deepening, until it seemed to her as though a great stake were being driven into her heart. And all the day the sensation would remain with her as of a heavy object burdening the place where this trouble lay. "Probably . . . very likely," she said to herself, "the next time I shall die of it." At the thought a wave of anticipation passed over her. "I shall probably die of it," she repeated cheerfully and became interested in some crayfish in the pool at her feet. She plucked some grasses behind her and started dragging them before the eyes of the indignant animals. "Nothing in life could make me abandon my sheep, but if I die they will have to fall back on Circumstance as I did. Glycerium, what will become of you? Apraxine, Mysis . . .? There are times when we cannot see one step ahead of us, but five years later we are eating and sleeping somewhere." (It was humorous, pretending that one's heart was as hard as that.) "Yes," she said aloud, to the pain that trembled within her, "only come quickly." She leaned forward still dragging the stems before the shellfish: "I have lived thirty-five years. I have lived enough. *Stranger, near this spot lies Chrysis, daughter of Arches of Andros: the ewe that has strayed from the flock lives many years in one day and dies at a great age when the sun sets.*" She laughed at the deceptive comforts of self-pity and taking off a sandal put her foot into the water. She drew herself up for a moment, asking herself what there was left in the house for the colony's supper; then recollecting some fish and some salad on the shelf, she returned to her thoughts. She repeated her epitaph, making it a song and emphasizing, for self-mockery, its false sentiment. "O Andros, O Poseidon, how happy I am. I have no right to be happy like this. . . ."

And she knew as she gazed at the frieze of dolphins still playing in the distance that her mind was avoiding another problem that awaited her. "I am happy because I love this Pamphilus,—Pamphilus the anxious, Pamphilus the stupid. Why cannot someone tell him that it is not necessary to suffer so about living." And the low exasperated sigh escaped her, the protest we make at the preposterous, the incorrigible beloved. "He thinks he is failing. He thinks he is inadequate to life at every turn. Let him rest some day, O ye Olympians, from pitying those who suffer. Let him learn to look the other way. This is something new in the world, this concern for the unfit and the broken. Once he begins that, there's no end to it, only madness. It leads nowhere. That is some god's business." Whereupon she discovered that she was weeping; but when she had dried her eyes she was still thinking about him. "Oh, such people are unconscious of their goodness. They strike their foreheads with their hands because of their failure, and yet the rest of us are made glad when we remember their faces. Pamphilus, you are another herald from the future. Some day men will be like you. Do not frown so. . . ."

But these thoughts were very fatiguing. She arose and, returning to the amphitheatre, laid herself down upon the sand. She murmured some fragments from the Euripidean choruses and fell asleep. She had always been an islander and this hot and impersonal sun playing upon a cold and impersonal sea was not unfriendly to her. And now for two hours the monotony of sun and sea played about her and wove itself into the mood of her sleeping mind. As once the gray-eyed Athena stood guarding Ulysses—she leaning upon her spear, her great heart full of concern and of those long divine thoughts that are her property—even so, now, the hour and the place all but gathered itself into a presence and shed its influence upon her. When her eyes finally opened she listened for a time to the calm in her heart. "Some day," she said, "we shall understand why we suffer. I shall be among the shades underground and some wonderful hand, some Alcestis, will touch me and will show me the meaning of all these things; and I shall laugh softly for hours as I do now . . . as I do now."

She arose and binding up her hair prepared to ascend the slope. But just as she turned to leave the place, there visited her the desire to do something ceremonial, to mark the hour. She stood up straightly and held out her arms to the setting sun: "If you still hear prayers from the lips of mortals, if our longings touch you at all, hear me now. Give to this Pamphilus some assurance—even some assurance such as you have given to me, unstable though I am—that he is right. And oh! (but I do not say this from vanity or pride, O Apollo,—but perhaps this is weak, this is childish of me, perhaps this renders the whole prayer powerless!) if it is possible, let the thought of me or of something I have said be comforting to him some day. And . . . and . . ."

But her arms fell to her side. The world seemed empty. The sun went down. The sea and sky became suddenly remote and she was left with only the tears in her eyes and the longing in her heart. She closed her lips and turned her head aside. "I suppose there is no god," she whispered. "We must do these things ourselves. We must drag ourselves through life as best we can."

❖   ❖   ❖

Chrysis had made the mistake of accustoming the members of her household to her invariable presence and now while she slept they became increasingly indignant at the length of her absence. In twos and threes they hovered about the door peering to the right and to the left with mingled scorn and alarm.

"When she comes in, see that no one says a word to her," directed Apraxine, a tall lame woman whom Chrysis had found beaten and left for dead at the edge of the desert below the terraces of Alexandria.

"Pretend you don't see her."

". . . to go sallying off a whole day without a word to a soul."

"I'm sure I don't wish to stay in a house where I count for nothing."

". . . less than nothing, it seems."

Presently however something happened that distracted their minds from their resentment. A new sheep arrived at the fold.

Simo's frank had carried to Andros the money that Chrysis intended for the support of the stricken sea-captain. But Philocles's guardians had long since tired of their charge and become discontented with the intermittent payments. They decided to take advantage of this sum of money to ship him off to Brynos. It was necessary for this purpose to wait for a lucid interval in the patient's condition. Such a moment finally arrived; they hurriedly made up his bundle, brushed his hair, and led him down to the water-front, where they found the captain of a boat sailing between the Cyclades who was willing to undertake the commission. And thus it was that on the afternoon of Chrysis's retreat to solitude Philocles arrived on Brynos. A boy who attended at one of the wineshops in the town was directed to escort him to her house, and suddenly the childlike sea-captain was thrust into the courtyard among the conspiring pensioners.

Ten years before Philocles had been the greatest navigator on the Mediterranean, first in skill and experience and

first in fame. He had been many times
to Sicily and to Carthage; he had passed
through the Gates of Hercules and visited
the Tyrian mines in Britain. He had
sailed westward for months across the
great shelf of water, seeking new islands,
and had been forced to turn back by the
visible anger of the gods. In the present
age men were captains or merchants or
farmers, but in the great age men had
been first Athenians or Greeks, and the
islanders regarded Philocles as of that
order, a belated giant. He was already
in middle life when Chrysis first knew
him—she had been a passenger on one of
his trips to Egypt—and it astonished her
to find someone laconic in a chattering
world and with quiet hands in a gestur-
ing civilization. He was blackened and
cured by all weathers. He stood in the
squares of the various ports of call, his

feet apart as though they were forever planted on a shifting deck. He seemed to be too large for daily life; his very eyes were strange—unaccustomed to the shorter range, too used to seizing the appearances of a constellation between a cloud and a cloud, and the outlines of a headland in rain. Wind, salt and starvation had moulded his head, and his mind had been rendered, not buoyant, but rich and concentrated by the enforced asceticisms of a prolonged duty and of long sea voyages. He had been one of the persons whom Chrysis had most loved in all her life and it was she who had discovered his secret, the secret that it was neither adventure nor gain that drove him along his adventurous life. He was passing the time and filling the hours in anticipation of release from a life that had lost its savor with the death of his daughter. These two saw in one another's eyes the thing they had in common, the fact that they had both died to themselves. They lived at one remove from that self that supports the generality of men, the self that is a bundle of self-assertions, of greeds, of vanities and of easily-offended pride. Three years before, Philocles had been forced to captain some ships of a city at war. He had been captured and mutilated and what was left of so kingly a person was a timorous child.

The sheep examined the newcomer who had been thrust so abruptly into their midst. They questioned him and amused themselves with his answers. Then they gave him a bench in the sunlight where he might whisper to his heart's content.

The sun set and soon after Chrysis came stumbling through the door, laughing apologetically and pushing back her hair. "Forgive me, O my dear friends, forgive me. I fell asleep on the sand and I'm very sorry I'm so late." (The men and women raised their eyebrows cynically and went on with their work.) "Apraxine, has anything happened?" (Apraxine cleared her throat with Alexandrian hauteur and became absorbed in looking for a thread on the ground.) "Now we must find something particularly rare for supper."

The sheep exchanged pitying glances over all this tawdry artifice and when Chrysis passed into the house they burst into laughter. The laughter was condescending, but the soul had returned to the community. Finally at a signal from Apraxine, Glycerium went to the door and announced to Chrysis that Philocles had arrived from Andros. He had seen her pass and some twinge of memory had set him trembling. He rose and walked unsteadily to the middle of the court. She saw him standing before her, haggard, with hollow puzzled eyes and with untrimmed beard.

She went forward repeating, "My dear friend, my friend!" but as she embraced him a loud voice within her seemed to say: "Something is going to happen. The threads of my life are drawing together."

❖ ❖ ❖

That night Chrysis was awakened from a light and feverish sleep by the instinctive knowledge that someone was near her. She raised herself on one elbow and peered towards the faint glimmer of the door.

"Who is it? Who is there?" she said.

A figure seemed suddenly to rise from the threshhold. "It's I, Chrysis. It's Glycerium."

"Is something the matter? Is someone ill?"

"No . . . it's only . . ."

"Light a lamp, my child. What do you want?"

"Chrysis, are you angry with me for waking you up? I couldn't sleep, Chrysis, and I had to come into your room."

"But why are you crying, my dear, my dove? Come now and sit on the edge of the bed. Of course I'm not angry with you." Glycerium sank upon the floor beside her. "No, no,—the floor is cold. Come sit up here. Your hair is wet! Tell me now, what is making you un-happy?"

"Nothing."

"What? Then you have something to tell me?"

"No . . . I don't know what . . . I just want you to talk to me."

"Well, I have something to tell you." Chrysis was stroking Glycerium's hair, delicately following with her finger-tips the strands as they passed above and behind the ear, when suddenly Glycerium threw her arms about her sister's neck and sobbed uncontrollably. Chrysis continued gravely with her caress, thinking that she was merely dealing with one of the meaningless accesses of despair that descend upon adolescence when the slow ache of existence is first apprehended by the growing mind. "There!" she murmured in a rhythmic undertone, "Sh . . . sh . . . sh . . . sh. . . . We love you. We all love you in this house. Our beautiful Glycerium, our gentle, our very beautiful

Glycerium . . . sh . . . sh . . . there! Are you comfortable now? I have some good news for you. (No, no, there is plenty of room.) This is it: Beginning tomorrow you are going to lead an altogether different life. I am going to let you wander all over the island alone. And when Mysis and I go to market you can go with us. You may climb the hills if you like, and you may explore along the water's edge,—I shall even show you the secret of the secrets of my heart,—a beautiful hidden shelter by the sea where one can be perfectly alone. . . . Well? are you pleased? Doesn't this news make you happy?"

"Yes, Chrysis."

"Now! I thought it would make you very happy and all you say is: Yes, Chrysis!"

"Chrysis, tell me: what will become of me?"

Chrysis changed her position and in the dark shut her eyes a moment. "Oh, my dear, my dear . . . that's what everyone asks, everyone on earth. Well, first you tell me: what do you want to become?"

"I want to marry someone and . . . and be in his home. Chrysis, tell me: can I marry someone? Without a father and a mother and without anything, is it possible that I can marry someone?"

"My dear, there is always . . ."

"Chrysis, I'm grown-up now. I'm fifteen. Please tell me the truth. I must know. Don't say something merely to quiet me. I must know the truth. Can a man ever ask me to marry him? Why are you waiting so long to answer me?"

"I have been planning to have a long talk with you about all these things. But not now. Wait a short time; wait

until you have had a week, two weeks,
of this new life when you will be free to
wander all over the island. Then you
will be able to understand better what I
have to say."

Glycerium paused a moment. "I know,
I know," she said, her face against
Chrysis's shoulder. "That means that
no one will ever be able to marry me."

"No, no, I don't say that. . . ."

Glycerium rose and stood in the middle
of the room. "I understand," she said
in the darkness.

Chrysis raised herself again on one
elbow and said slowly: "We are not
Greek citizens. We are not people with
homes. We are considered strange, only
a little above the slaves. All those others
live in homes and everyone knows their
fathers and their mothers; they marry
one another. They think we would

never fit into their life. Although all that is true,—"

"But there are stories," said Glycerium, "of men who even married girls that had been slaves."

"Yes, if a young man should fall in love with you, it is possible that he would take you into his home. That is why I have tried to take such care of you and why I have kept you hidden here in the house. Through the young men who come to the banquets, the island knows that you are here and that you have been carefully protected. And now that you are to walk about the island freely you must be a hundred times more careful than other girls. You are beautiful and you are good, and before all their unfriendly eyes you must show them your modesty and your goodness. That is all there is to say and to hope, my child."

"Perhaps, Chrysis . . . it is best that I do not go about the island freely, after all."

"No, no. You will feel like going out. It will come gradually. But now you must go to bed and to sleep, my darling. All these things will solve themselves as best they can. All you can do for the present is to be yourself, your very self, my Glycerium."

Glycerium moved unsteadily towards the bed: "Chrysis, I must tell you something."

"Yes? . . ."

"You will be angry with me, Chrysis."

"Why . . ."

"May the gods protect me, I . . . I have been talking with Mysis and now I know that I am going to be the mother of a child."

There was silence for a moment followed by the sound of Chrysis putting her feet upon the floor. "Where is Mysis? Let me get up."

"It is true, Chrysis. I broke my promise the times when you were away. I used to go out over the hills."

"Oh, my child, my child!"

"But he loves me. He will marry me. He loves me, I know."

"Who is it? What is his name?"

"It is Pamphilus, son of Simo."

Chrysis grew rigid in the darkness. Then she slowly put her feet back into the bed. Glycerium continued wildly: "He loves me. He will take care of me. He has told me so a hundred times. Chrysis, what shall I do? What shall I do? I am afraid."

A low moan at the door revealed the fact that Mysis had accompanied her younger mistress to this interview and was kneeling outside the door without the courage to enter.

After a moment Chrysis said in a light impersonal voice: "Well, you . . . go off to bed now and go to sleep. Yes. We'll both be catching cold here. It's late. I think it must be almost morning."

"I cannot sleep."

"Everything will be all right, Glycerium. I can't talk any more now. I'm not well. We'll talk about it in the morning."

Glycerium left the room, trembling.

In her darker hours Chrysis carried on what she called a "dialogue with Fate." And now as she turned to the wall she said: "I hear you. You have won again."

Before long the pain in her side became fixed and unremitting, and Chrysis knew that her life was drawing to a close. She

took to her bed and her thoughts no
longer clung to the world about her. Now
when her courage was being undermined
by her pain she dared not ask herself if
she had lived and if she were dying, un-
loved, in disorder, without meaning.
From time to time she peered into her
mind to ascertain what her beliefs were
in regard to a life after death, its judg-
ments or its felicities; but the most ex-
hausting of all our adventures is that
journey down the long corridors of the
mind to the last halls where belief is en-
throned. She resigned herself to the
memory of certain moments when in-
tuition had comforted her and she quieted
her heart with Andrian cradle-songs and
with fragments from the tragic poets.
She saved her strength to fulfill a last
desire, one that may perhaps seem un-
worthy to persons of a later age. Her

mind had been moulded by formal literature, by epics and odes, by tragedies and by heroic biography, and from this reading she had been imbued with the superstition that one should die in a noble manner, and in this high decorum even the maintenance of her beauty played a part. The only terror left in the world was the fear that she might leave it with cries of pain, with a torn mind, and with discomposed features.

The news spread about the island that the Andrian was gravely ill. The young men who had been her guests were confused by the discrepancy between their mothers' sarcasms and the respect that Chrysis had inspired in themselves, but some brought shy offerings of wine and cheese to her door. For such brief interviews she raised herself on one elbow and

sought to recover her light-spoken gra-
ciousness. But most of the young men
stayed away; it required a maturer mind
than they could summon to hold side by
side their memories of sensual pleasure
and their respect due to the dying.

Pamphilus had other reasons for stay-
ing away. It seemed more and more un-
likely that he would ever be permitted to
marry Glycerium. But one morning he
appeared at Chrysis's house and asked
to see her. He traversed the court, pick-
ing his way among her motley and dis-
mayed pensioners, and his eyes fell upon
Glycerium. She was seated beside Philocles at her sister's door, silent and
without hope. Pamphilus stopped for a
moment on one knee before her and took
her hands in his. "Do not be afraid," he
said in a low voice. "No harm will come
to you." She derived no courage from

his words; she lifted her eyes and scanned his face. Her mouth trembled, but no words came and her eyes returned to the ground. Pamphilus passed into the room where Chrysis lay; for a moment he could distinguish nothing in the darkness. Presently he became aware of the priest of Æsculapius and Apollo bending over a brazier in the corner, and finally he saw Chrysis smiling at him gravely from the bed. He sat down beside her in silence; each waited for the other to begin.

"We are sorry, all of us are sorry, Chrysis," he said at last, "to hear that you have been so ill."

"Thank you, Pamphilus. Thank them all."

"There . . . there has been so much rain. When the sunlight returns you will feel better at once."

"Yes, it has always been the sunlight

that has done me the most good. You are all well on your farm?"

"Yes, the gods be praised."

"The gods be praised. I shall never forget a favor your father did for me."

Pamphilus was struck with amazement. "My father?"

"Oh, forgive me . . . I remember now I promised him not to mention it to you. Oh, my illness has made me forget that. I am ashamed, I am ashamed. But now I had better add that it was a small commission he did for me by one of his boats going to Andros. I would not have him think me unfaithful to my promise. I beg of you earnestly not to tell him that I spoke of it."

"Indeed, I shall not tell him, Chrysis."

There fell another pause between them, while her strengthless hands lightly pressed upon the bed in her self-reproach.

"Yes," said Pamphilus. "When there is more sunlight you will feel better at once. The sky has been overcast for a long time. I cannot remember when it has been overcast so long."

To themselves they both cried: "How shall we ever get out of this?"

"We have missed the banquets. I would like to tell you again, Chrysis, what great pleasure they gave me. I have been looking forward to the next one when you promised to read us I forget what play."

"It was to have been the *Ion* of Euripides."

"Yes."

"This," said Chrysis, glancing towards the priest with a smile, "this is my Ion."

But perhaps the words were ill-chosen. She thought she saw the priest frowning as he bent over his work. "Forgive me," she said to him abruptly, "if I have offended you. I did not mean it ill."

But the tears were rolling down her cheeks. "Life, Pamphilus," she said, "is full of mistakes, but the wrongs we do to those we love and honor are more than we can endure." The priest approached the further side of the bed and adjusted the pillows; he whispered a few words into her ear and went back to his brazier.

"Am I tiring you?" Pamphilus asked.

"No, no. I am very happy that you have come." To herself she thought: "Time is passing, and what are we saying! Is there not something heartfelt that I can find to say to him, something to remember, for him and for me?" But she distrusted the emotion that filled her heart. It was perhaps mere excitement

and pain; or a vague and false sentiment. Probably the best thing to do
was to be stoic; to be brave and in-
articulate; to talk of trivial things. Or
was it a greater bravery to surmount
this shame and to say whatever obvious
words the heart dictated? Which was
right?

Pamphilus was thinking: "She is dying. What can I say to her? But I have
never been able to place words rightly.
I am dull. I am nothing to her but the
man who has wronged her sister." Aloud
he said in a low voice: "I shall marry
Glycerium if I can, Chrysis. At all
events you may be sure that no harm
will come to her."

"Though I love her dearly," replied
Chrysis, finding her words with great
difficulty "I shall not urge you. I . . . I
no, longer believe that what happens to

us is important. You will marry Glycerium or another. The years will unfold
these things. It is the life in the mind
that is important."

"I shall do what I can for her."

"You have only to be yourself without
fear, without doubting, Pamphilus."

"Chrysis, you will forgive me for having spoken to you so little at the banquets . . . and for having sat at the further
end and . . . that is the way I am. It
was not because I did not respect you.
I cannot talk as those others can. I am
only a listener. Even now I cannot say
what I mean. But I followed all that
you said."

The pain in Chrysis's side seemed to
increase beyond all endurance. "Oh,
friend," she said, "do not distrust. These
things are not so unsatisfactory . . . so
interrupted as they seem to be." The

priest had been watching her; she made a slight sign to him. "I do not wish you to go away," she continued to Pamphilus, almost in a whisper, "but it is best that I sleep now." Then raising herself on one elbow she breathed in anguish: "Perhaps we shall meet somewhere beyond life when all these pains shall have been removed. I think the gods have some mystery still in store for us. But if we do not, let me say now . . ." her hands opened and closed upon the cloths that covered her, ". . . I want to say to someone . . . that I have known the worst that the world can do to me, and that nevertheless I praise the world and all living. All that is, is well. Remember some day, remember me as one who loved all things and accepted from the gods all things, the bright and the dark. And do you likewise. Farewell."

THE WOMAN

Simo arose early to witness Chrysis's funeral. The Greeks, for reasons that lay deep in their sense of the fitness of things and in their superstition, conducted their funerals in the hour before dawn, and it was therefore still profound night when the little procession of her household prepared to pass through the streets of the town. When Simo arrived at the square he found that many of the men of Brynos had already gathered there and, drawing the folds of their rough cloaks about them, were standing talking together in low voices. The men of his own age had brought their curiosity and contempt with them and were congratulating themselves on the island's happy deliverance from the foreign woman; but the younger men who had known Chrysis stood with sullen faces, their throats rigid with antagonism at the glee of their elders.

Simo took his place in silence beside Chremes, but refused to respond to the latter's animated comment. Presently as the sounds of the flute and the mourners were heard approaching he discovered Pamphilus standing beside him, as silent as himself.

Mysis herded the shuffling and stumbling company before her as best she could. Philocles walked with lifted knees, as children do in a procession. In one hand he held some grasses and with the other he clutched the mantle of his companion, the old doorkeeper; but he was continually straying off, or standing still to gaze with wide dazzled eyes at the torches that preceded him or at the laughing by-standers. Behind him the deaf and dumb Ethiopian girl could scarcely be restrained from running forward to walk beside her sleeping friend,

Chrysis, whose rebuke had been so terrible when she had done wrong and whose smile had been sufficient compensation for her imprisonment in silence. Glycerium walked with lowered eyes, lost to hope and lost to the decorum that now required of her the wailing and the distraught gestures of a conspicuous mourner. All these passed forward under the bright stars that had received the first intimation of day and shone with a last heightened brilliance, and under the long garlands of smoke that hung above the company in that windless air.

As the onlookers accompanied the procession into the open country, Simo's attention was fixed upon Glycerium, by reason of her condition, which was apparent to all, of her resemblance to her sister, of the dejection that invested her, and of the beauty and modesty of her

bearing. And he became aware that his
son also was watching the girl. In fact,
during the whole journey, Pamphilus
bent upon her his burning eyes, trying
to intercept her glance and to communi-
cate to her his encouragement and his
love. But not until they reached the
heaped-up wood whereon the bodies of
a goat and a lamb were laid beside that
of Chrysis, and not until the fire had
touched it, did she raise her eyes. Then
as the sound of the wailing increased in
shrillness and the sound of the flute
floated piercingly above all, she turned
to Mysis and began to speak wildly into
her ear. But the words of her vehemence
were not heard in that din, nor were
Mysis's words of encouragement. Glycerium was trying to draw herself away
from the supporting arm of the other
and the slow faltering struggle of the

two women was lighted up by the rising flames. Pamphilus, in the intensity of his concentration upon the suffering of the girl, moved slowly forward, his hands held out before him. And now he heard the words that she was repeating: "It's best. It's best so!" Suddenly Glycerium pushed the older woman away from her and with a loud cry of "Chrysis!" stumbled forward to fling herself upon the body of her sister.

But Pamphilus had foreseen this attempt. Running across the sand, he seized her by her disheveled hair and drew her back and into his arms. The touch of that encircling arm released her tears. She laid her head against his breast as one who had been there before and was returning home.

The scandal of this embrace was felt at once by all the by-standers and chiefly by Chremes, who turned upon Simo with his protest and astonishment. But Simo had moved away and was walking slowly home through the breaking dawn. Now he understood the Pamphilus of the last months.

The islanders discussed interminably the surprising event that had taken place at Chrysis's funeral. They watched with hushed excitement the chill that had fallen across the relations between the families of Simo and of Chremes. Rumor presently asserted that Pamphilus had promised to acknowledge the child, though no one, naturally, even discussed the possibility of a marriage. Readers of a later age will not be able to understand the difficulties that beset the young man. Marriage was not then a sentimental relation, but a legal one of great dignity, and the bridegroom's share in the

contract involved not so much himself
as his family, his farm, and his ancestors.
Without the support of his parents and
without a residence in their home a young
man was a mere adventurer, without
social, economic or civil standing. A
marriage was only possible if Simo declared it to be so. The customs of the
islands encouraged fathers in the luxuries
of blustering and tyranny, but Simo's
relations with his son had always been
strangely impersonal. He was confused
by his own deference for his son, by what
he thought was his own weakness. Yet
Simo's silence did not have the air of a
final refusal; it even seemed to imply
that the decision, with all its possibilities
of lifetime regret and of a lifetime's con-
tention on the farm, rested with Pamphilus.

One day several months after Chrysis's

funeral Pamphilus betook himself to the palaestra for some exercise. He entered the low door and, nodding to a group of friends that sat scuffling under an awning at the edge of the enclosure, he walked across the hot red sand. The old attendant at the door who had won a laurel wreath in his youth came trotting across the burning ring after him and as soon as Pamphilus had seated himself on a marble bench began kneading his calves and ankles. In the centre of the field Chremes's son was going through the motions of hurling an imaginary discus; thirty and fifty times he turned with lifted knee, trying to fix in his muscular memory the perfect synchronization of the gestures. Two other young men were practicing a festival dance, interrupting their work from time to time to criticize one another's slightest deviation from a

harmonious balance. The young priest
of Æsculapius and Apollo was running
around the course. Pamphilus sent the
attendant away and lying down on his
cloak let the sunlight beat upon him.
He did not think about his problem, but
left his mind a blank, suffused with a
dull misery that identified itself with the
drowsy heat. Presently he placed his
elbow on the ground and raising his head
rested his cheek upon his hand and
watched the priest of Apollo.

The priest never entered the competi-
tive games, but he was undoubtedly first
upon the island for endurance and second
only to Pamphilus in swiftness. Save on
the days of festival he appeared for exercise daily and ran six miles. He preserved
a perfect temperance: he drank no wine;
he lived on fruit and vegetables; he awoke
with the sun and unless there was some

call to attend the sick he went to sleep
with it. He had taken the vow of chas-
tity, the vow that forever closes the mind
to the matter, without wistful back-
glancing and without conceding the possibility that circumstance might yet present
a harmless deviation, the vow which,
when profoundly compassed, fills the
mind with such power that it is forever
cut off from the unstable tentative sons
of men. His office required his passing
so much time among the sick and the
distressed that he had become inadequate
to the cheerful and the happy and no one
on the island knew him very well. But
he had a strange power over the sick and
the demented and only in their hours of
confession and despair was the shutter of
his impersonality lifted; such as had
known him then followed him ever after
with their eyes, in gratitude and in as-

tonishment. He was only twenty-eight, but he had been sent to Brynos by the priests that attended the great mysteries of Athens and Corinth as a signal honor; for the shrine on Brynos was one of particular significance in the legend of Æsculapius and his father Apollo. Pamphilus had never spoken to him beyond the salutations of the field, but he would rather have known him than anyone in the world, and he in turn watched Pamphilus with grave interest. Now Pamphilus lay following him with his eyes and wishing he had his own life to live over again.

Suddenly he became aware that someone was shaking him by the shoulder. It was one of his companions. "Here comes your father," said the boy and went back to the awning. Pamphilus rose to his feet and waited respectfully as Simo approached, preceded by the old attendant.

"Stay where you are. Lie down again," said Simo; "I'll sit here on this bench. I want to talk to you."

Pamphilus lay down, his face turned away towards the track.

Simo wiped his face with the hem of his skirt. "I won't be long, my boy. . . . But we must consider this matter somehow . . . after all." He was not sure of himself. He blew his nose. He coughed several times and roughly adjusted the folds of his gown. He repeated "Very well" and "Now" and waited in vain for Pamphilus to say something. At last he launched forth among his prepared introductions:

"Well now, my boy, I assume you want to marry the girl. Hm . . ."

Pamphilus put his head down between

his folded arms as though he were going to sleep. He sighed in anticipation of all the irrelevancies he was about to hear. In his heart he knew he had only to say yes or no and his father would accede to his wish.

"I don't wish to coerce you. I think you are old enough to see the good and the bad for yourself. But for a few moments now I want to talk all around the matter. I want to put the other side of the case in its plainest terms and leave it there for a while. May I do that?"

"Yes," said Pamphilus.

"Well, to begin with, it's only right to face the fact that there is no outward obligation to marry the girl. I've looked into the matter. She is not a Greek citizen. She happens to have been brought up in a sheltered manner, or so I take it. This Chrysis seems to have tried to prevent the girl's falling into her way of life; but that does not alter the fact that she is a mere dancing girl. Now, mind you, I can see that she is modest and well-mannered. She appears to be just such a person as our own Argo. But she could never have hoped for anything above the situation she is now in. The world is full of just such likable stray girls as this Glycerium, but we cannot be expected to welcome them into the fabric of good Greek family life. You may be sure that Chrysis knew perfectly well that Glycerium must some day become a hetaira like herself, or a servant."

Simo paused. He could see the back only of his son's head, but he was able to imagine upon his face the set unhappy expression they had all been obliged to watch there for the last weeks. He coughed again and abruptly flung himself upon another of his openings:

"No doubt you feel yourself fairly bound to her by a promise—but a promise, Pamphilus, in which you failed to consider the rest of us, and especially your mother. If you decided to marry the girl, your mother and sister would try to live with her as peaceably as possible, we know; but it would be a good deal to ask of them. You know them. This girl does not understand the first thing about our island manners. She doesn't know how simple and monotonous our women's lives are. I expect that life with the Andrian and with that strange company at the house on the hill was an odd affair. She'd be unhappy with us. And even if she didn't contradict your mother all day . . . and worse . . . she'd become silent and sullen. Pamphilus, they would never grow fond of one another. It would be better to be cruel to

her now and let her alone, than to set up
discord, a lifetime of discord on our farm."

For a moment his memory failed him,
but he rallied and continued:

"Well, even assuming that your mother
and sister came to like her and to accept
her cordially in the home, all her life she
would have to endure something insulting
in the manner of the other women on the
island. We men do not take that interest
in social discrimination, my son, but
women . . . women with their few inter-
ests and . . . and so on . . . they enjoy
having someone to ignore or to stare
down. It warms them. Glycerium is
not a Greek citizen. Her sister was a
hetaira. All her life she would be obliged
to endure their looking at her with
straight lips and (I can see them) with
half-closed eyes. But even that is not
the chief thing."

THE WOMAN

He hoped that the suspense in this splendid transition would be reflected in some change in his son's position, but the young man lay motionless. Simo's weary eyes turned slowly about the palaestra.

"The girl is not strong. The women of the village seem to know something about it. She's a quick nervous high-strung girl and she'd bring you a series of thin and sickly children. You and I know those homes. She's not unlike our neighbor Douro's wife; isn't she? and the uneven health of such women—even though they're often more likable, yes, more likable, than the Philumenas— takes the shape of complaining and quarrelsomeness. And in their children. One has no right to bring into the world those children that cannot join others in their games, silent children who go through life regularly subject to fevers and coughs and pains. The most important thing in life is a houseful of strong healthy boys. Take Philumena, now. You do not 'love' Philumena, as the poets use the word. Well, when I married your mother perhaps I did not 'love' her in that sense. But I grew to love her and . . . euh . . . now I cannot imagine myself as having been married to anyone else, as satisfactorily married to anyone else. Philumena is handsome. But most important of all, Philumena is strong. So . . . so, Pamphilus, does what I am saying seem to have some truth in it? . . . Pamphilus?"

But Pamphilus had fallen asleep.

His last thought had been the recollection of one of Chrysis's maxims, an ironic phrase which he had chosen to take literally: *The mistakes we make*

*through generosity are less terrible than the
gains we acquire through caution.*

Simo was not vexed. He sighed.
Looking up he saw the priest of Æsculapius and Apollo running around the
course. He recalled the day several
months before when he and Sostrata had
taken Pamphilus's sister to the temple.
For two days and two nights, Argo had
been suffering from an ear-ache, and although they knew that the priest was
often ungracious when his attention was
asked on smaller ills they ventured to
present her to him. The hour at which
he was accustomed to receive the sick
was a little after sunrise and there they
found his colony. There were invalids
brought to him on beds; there were suf-
ferers from tumors, from protracted lan-
guors, from sore eyes; there were the
possessed. Simo and Sostrata had passed

their lives without ailments. They regarded them, like poverty, like unclean-
liness, as mere bad citizenship; they
were on the point of returning home, so
great was their distaste for such manifestations. The priest required that the
guardians who had brought their sick to
him should retire to a distance during
his interviews, and Simo and Sostrata
had withdrawn with an ill grace to a
nearby grove. Argo seemed not to share
her parents' revulsion from these matters;
even before she approached the place
(her fingers pressed upon her ear) she had
been subdued to awe and when her turn
came she told her little story with caught
breath. The priest gently touched her
ear, reciting a charm. He poured in
some oil and looked deeply into her shy
eyes. And gradually as he gazed at her
a smile appeared upon his lips and slowly

she smiled in return. True influence over
another comes not from a moment's eloquence nor from any happily chosen
word, but from the accumulation of a
lifetime's thoughts stored up in the eyes.
And there is one thing greater than cur-
ing a malady and that is accepting a
malady and sharing its acceptance. The
ear-ache did not abate at once, but Argo
pretended to her parents that it did, for
the other healing they would not have
understood; and all night long instead of
complaining she pressed against her ear
the little bag of laurel leaves he had given
her and talked to herself, rehearsing that
interview and that glance. Thereafter
she never had any conversation with the
priest, but when she happened to meet
him upon the road, her heart was filled
with excitement; she gave him a shy
greeting and her eyelids fluttered in a

quick intimate glance and he in turn let fall upon her a faint allusion to his smile. Her parents were amused by this bond; the priest had brought out in their daughter a side they had never known in her, and one that sent messages all along her life. Henceforth she even stood up straighter. One day a cousin who lived on the other side of the island came to a meal with them and let fall a remark in disparagement of the priest, saying that he was a comfort chiefly to old women who imagined themselves to be ill. Argo's eyes grew dark and her lips straight with anger. She refused to eat another mouthful and forever after the poor foolish cousin could never draw a word from her and never knew why. All this now returned to Simo's mind as he watched the priest.

"People like that," he thought to himself, "have some secret about living. Why don't they tell it to us outright, instead of wrapping it up in mystery and ceremonial? They know something that prevents their blundering about, as we do. Yes, what am I doing here," he added, pushing out his lower lip, "but playing the fool? Blundering, advising in things I know nothing about." He looked long at his sleeping son. "Pamphilus has some of that secret, too. And that woman from Andros had it, too. Chremes was right, though he meant it ill: there is something of the priest in Pamphilus, something of the priest trying to make its way in him. Let me get up and go away before I say anything more."

So he arose and a little guiltily left the field.

Pamphilus's mind was all but made up,

yet still under the burden of perplexity and self-reproach he decided to seek still more light on his problem and a last reassurance by reviving a custom that had been in frequent use among the Greeks of the great age, but which had fallen off at the time of the events of this story. It consisted merely in abstaining from speech and from food from one sunrise to the next and in either passing the night in the temple enclosure or in arriving there before the dawn that closed the watch. There was not thought to be any particular magic in the practice: it cleared the mind of bodily fumes, it removed it from the commerce of the day and prepared it perhaps for a significant dream. The watcher guarded his fast and his silence, but the Greek mind did not approve of heightening the experience by any further self-denial. One moved about

the home as usual, exercised in the palaestra or worked at the loom; one slept.
If some uninformed person spoke to the
watcher, he drew his finger across his
lips and the condition of the vow was
understood. Athletes still observed it
several days before a race; brides on the
eve of their wedding; old ladies who
hoped to recover some lost trinket, or to
recapture in a dream the features of some
all-but-forgotten love; and devout soldiers
about to set forth upon an expedition.
It was indeed little short of odd that a
healthy young man in the even current
of life should revive this custom, but the
islanders were still sufficiently religious
to respect the habits that had expressed
the spiritual life of their glorious grand-
fathers, and made no comment.

By mid-afternoon hunger had gained
upon him and his dejection had increased

a hundred-fold. Whichever choice he made would involve the unhappiness of others. Under the weight of the alternatives even the memory of Glycerium lost for a time any tender association. He climbed over the remoter parts of the island, gazing absently out to sea and idly plucking the grasses among the rocks where he sat. He came to the spot where he had first seen Glycerium and stood for a time, quiet as the stones about him, asking himself whether the associations in life are based upon an accidental encounter or upon a profound and inner necessity. When he returned to the farm his mother and sister felt the desolation that invested him and moved about with hushed steps. The very slaves went about their tasks on tiptoe and finally withdrew in silence and in alarmed interrogation. During the evening meal Pam-

philus sat by the door with closed eyes.
His brother, returning, stepped over his
feet with awed circumspection (he too
had made the watch only a few months
before, but in pomp, with twelve other
youths on the occasion of their enroll-
ment in the League) and held himself at
a distance, rendered uncomfortable by
so much seriousness in a good athlete.
Of her own accord Argo brought Pamphilus a bowl of water which he drank,
smiling the while intimately into her
grave eyes; she returned to her place at
the table with great dignity and with
secret excitement, as though she had
done something conspicuous. When Simo
finally told her and her brother to go to
bed she slipped up to her father and laid
her lips against his ear: "What is it,
father?" she whispered. "No, tell me,
what is the matter?" He took her hands

and played with them a moment; he raised his eyebrows wisely and told her to go to bed and sleep well. From her bed in the darkness she noted the movements of the family: that her mother took a cloak and went out into the garden by the cliff, and that later her father did the same. With wide eyes and cautious lifted ear she followed this unaccustomed nocturnal roaming. She was filled with loving excitement; she kissed her doll many times with violence and wept. She became aware that her younger brother was venturing on hands and knees towards the moonlight in the court: she too ventured out and they stared at one another, but Pamphilus suddenly loomed up from the shadows and waved them back to their beds.

Pamphilus wandered about the outer court. Again the moon was at the full,

throwing a milky blue mist over the tiers
of olive trees that climbed the hill across
the road and casting black shadows
among the farm buildings. Its serenity
contrasted strangely with the mysterious
excitement it awakened among the human
beings it fell upon. Pamphilus had seen
his parents go into the garden, but he
saw them now without emotion, without
pity. He returned to the house and lay
down upon his bed. Never had he been
possessed by mood further from illumina-
tion. Lying on his face he traced outlines
upon the floor with his finger.

The shells gleamed on the path as
Simo walked up and down; from time
to time he cast a furtive glance at his
wife. She was sitting on a bench of
chipped and stained marble that had been
his mother's favorite seat. It had been
placed there generations before, under a

fig arbor blown down long since on a night of legendary storm. It stood at the very end of the garden where a cliff broke down to the sea, and from it one could hear forever the long spreading whispers of the ebbing and the rising waves below. From that seat his mother had directed the bringing up of five children, had dried their tears and listened with nodding head to the absurd procession of their shifting enthusiasms. "Viewed from a distance," Simo said to himself, "life is harmonious and beautiful. No doubt the years when my mother smiled to us from that bench were as full of crossed wills and exasperations as today, but how beautiful they seem in memory! The dead are wrapped in love; in illusion, perhaps. They go underground and slowly this tender light begins to fall upon them. But the pres-

ent remains: this succession of small do-
mestic vexations. I have lived such a life
for sixty years and I am still upset by its
ephemeral decisions. And I am still
asking myself which is the real life: the
present with its discontent, or the retro-
spect with its emotion?" He looked again
guardedly at Sostrata, who sat fingering
the folds of her cloak and expressing in
every line of her position her unfriendli-
ness and her rebellion. "The fault is in
me," he continued. "If I were wiser, I
could do this thing. As the head of the
family I should be firmer. I should say
'yes' or 'no' clearly and let Pamphilus
bring in his little girl. I should weed out
all these hesitations. Even now she is
waiting for me to make up her mind for
her; if I spoke distinctly, even against
her will, she would adjust herself without
great effort. The house would find a way

of accepting the new member and things would run on smoothly enough." He was thinking of going towards her with smiling affection, suggesting that at sixty they had earned the right to remain tranquil though the house fell; but he foresaw that her pride would not accommodate itself to any such resignation, and he continued up and down the garden.

Indeed Sostrata did not wish Simo to speak to her. Her mind was filled with one long obstinate exclamation at the stupidity of men. Only a woman's mind could foresee all the harm that would result from such a marriage as the one now being weighed. It was the women of the island that had measured all danger that came with the arrival of the Alexandrian woman; and now she, the first matron of Brynos, was being ordered to receive into her home the last offscouring of that dispersed colony. She had anticipated all her life the rich satisfactions of being a mother-in-law and a grandmother, though what she anticipated was a daughter-in-law of straw. A Greek HOME, she knew, was the only breakwater against the tide of oriental manners, of financial fluctuation, and of political chaos. The highest point towards which any existence could aspire was to be a member of an island family, living and dying on one farm, respected, cautious, and secretly wealthy; of a family stretching into the past as far as the mossy funerary urns could record, and into the future as far as the imagination could reach, that is to one's grandchildren. Society was similarity. These things she repeated to herself, and under the waves of her indignation and self-pity—though the greater part of the time she stood in awe of her

husband and her son—all her gracious
traits disappeared, her beautiful eyes became harsh that for three days had been
bright with the angry tears of her inner
monologue.

When after a long stretch of time Simo
paused in his walk and approached her
with deferential hesitation, she arose
abruptly and walked past him into the
house, breathing hard and trembling with
excitement.

At last Pamphilus arose and throwing
his fleece-lined cloak over his shoulder
slowly and musingly walked through the
little garden in the court and passed
through the outer gates of the farm. He
was strangely light-headed from hunger
and dejection. He paused for a moment
to gaze at the rising hillside before him
and its silvered olive trees. To his eyes
they seemed to be pulsating in even waves

of intensity, as though the whole earth
and sky were on fire and burning with a
pale slow silver flame, the whole earth
and sky, unconsumed yet incessantly
feeding the countless tongues of flame.
He was gazing at this serene conflagra-
tion when he became aware of two dim
figures in a pool of profound shadow at
his right, leaning against the pillar of the
gate. Glycerium was pressing her cheek
against the stone and breathing her
prayer towards the house within and beside her Mysis, distraught and helpless,
stood urging her mistress to return home
and to leave the ominous vapors of the
night and the jealous chill of the moon.

When Glycerium saw that Pamphilus
was standing in the road and that he
had recognized her, she drew back into
Mysis's arms overcome with shame; but
slowly collecting herself she stretched

forward a hand to him and fixed her great eyes imploringly on his face.

Mysis whispered to her: "We must go home, my bird, my treasure."

"Pamphilus," said Glycerium, "help me!"

His heart contracted within him as he realized the extremity of suffering that had led her thus far. He laid his finger gravely across his lips. He did not smile, but approaching her he looked down into her face with earnest reassurance and beckoned her to accompany Mysis toward the town.

Glycerium pushed back the scarf from her forehead and fell upon one knee before him, babbling incoherently: "I love you. I love you, Pamphilus. You promised me that you loved me. What am I to do? What is to become of me?"

Pamphilus looked at Mysis and again drew his finger across his mouth.

"Hush, my darling," she said. "You see he has taken the vow and cannot speak to us. And we must not speak to him. Look, he wants you to start home with me." She put her arm about the girl's waist and they began to move slowly toward the road.

"He promised me that he loved me," muttered Glycerium, unable to see for her tears, but permitting herself to be led forward. After a few steps, however, she turned and, pushing Mysis aside, said: "No, no! I wish to see him again." She pressed her scarf against her mouth for a moment and gazed at him, her whole soul in her eyes: "Pamphilus, do not marry me, if it is not right. But do not leave me alone. Do not leave me so long alone. Remember Chrysis. Remember the day you found me being stoned by the boys. No, no, do not marry me, if your father and your mother do not wish it, but let me know that . . . that I am still loved by you."

At last he nodded and smiled and waved to her slowly.

"He is nodding his head, Mysis!" cried Glycerium.

"Yes, my treasure."

"Look, Mysis, he is smiling at me. Can you see? Look very hard, Mysis."

"See, now he is waving to you. Wave to him again."

Glycerium waved eagerly, like a child, until Pamphilus was out of sight. It was a long walk home over uneven stones. Glycerium talked excitedly of the smile, trying to estimate the exact shade of intention and affection that lay in his waving to her and in the nod of his head. They discussed the significance of his taking the vow and they talked in general of the custom of taking the vow and recalled all the occasions they could remember of this usage and the results of each occasion. "All will be well, Mysis," she repeated feverishly. "You will see, believe me, all will be well." But finally they fell silent, and in the silence their fears returned and an overwhelming weariness. As they reached the door of their house, Glycerium paused with tight-drawn lower lip and with fear in her eyes: "There is nothing to hope for," she said. "The gods are angry because I thought for a time that I was happy and that the world was easy to live in. At that time I did not understand anything about life and I said cruel things to Chrysis, because I thought the world was easy to live in. And the gods are right. Oh, if I could speak to her for only one moment and could tell her that now I

understand her goodness, her goodness.
But Chrysis is dead!" She turned to
Mysis, but at these words Mysis had
withdrawn from her and, beating upon
her forehead with the knuckles of her two
hands, had fallen upon the threshold of
the house.

❖　❖　❖

Pamphilus continued in the opposite
direction. He wandered about the up-
land pastures as he had done all day, and
climbed to the highest point on the island
to gaze upon the moon and the sea. He
tried to lift his mind out of the narrow
situation of his problem by thinking of
things not before him. He thought of
the ships that under that magical flowing

light were making their way from port
to port, each one casting aside at its prow
two glistening murmurous waves. It was
the hour when the helmsman in the se-
curity of the course falls into a reverie,
remembers his childhood or reckons up
his savings. Pamphilus thought of the
thousands of homes over all Greece where
sleeping or waking souls were forever
turning over the dim assignment of life.
"Lift every roof," as Chrysis used to say,
"and you will find seven puzzled hearts."
He thought of Chrysis and her urn, and
remembered her strange command to him
that he praise all life, even the dark. And
as he thought of her his depression, like
a cloud, drifted away from him and he
was filled with a tremulous happiness.
He too praised the whole texture of life,
for he saw how strangely life's richest
gift flowered from frustration and cruelty

and separation. Chrysis living and Chrysis dying in pain; the thoughtful glance that his father so often let rest upon him and the weary expression on his father's face when he thought himself unobserved; the shy mystery of Glycerium. It seemed to him that the whole world did not consist of rocks and trees and water nor were human beings garments and flesh, but all burned, like the hillside of olive trees, with the perpetual flames of love,—a sad love that was half hope, often rebuked and waiting to be reassured of its truth. But why then a love so defeated, as though it were waiting for a voice to come from the skies, declaring that therein lay the secret of the world. The moonlight is intermittent and veiled, and it was under such a light that they lived; but his heart suddenly declared to him that a sun would rise and before that

sun the timidity and the hesitation would
disappear. And as he strode forward this
truth became clearer and clearer to him
and he laughed because he had been so
long blind to what was so obvious. He
strode forward, his arms raised to the
sky in joyous gratitude, and as he went
he cried: "I praise all living, the bright
and the dark."

The exhilaration gave place finally to
a tranquil fatigue. As he entered the
shadowy temple he saw the priest sleeping before the altar he tended. The priest
opened his eyes a moment and above the
curve of his arm he watched the young
man spread his cloak upon the marble
pavement and lie down upon it and fall
asleep.

❖ ❖ ❖

Simo was awakened a little before dawn by the sounds of shrill voices and of unaccustomed movement in the outer courtyard. On approaching he discovered that a clamorous old woman had entered the gates and that a number of his slaves were trying in vain to quiet her and to drive her back into the road. He recognized Mysis. With a gesture he commanded the men to release her. "What is the matter?" he asked.

"I must see Pamphilus."

"He is not here."

"I cannot go away until I have seen him," she replied, her voice rising in feverish insistence. "A life depends upon it. I do not care what happens to me, but Pamphilus must know what they have done to us."

Simo said quietly: "I shall have you whipped; I shall have you shut up in a room for three days, if you continue to make this noise. Pamphilus will be able to listen to you later in the morning."

Mysis was silent a moment, then she raised her eyes and said sombrely: "Later in the morning will be too late, and all will be lost. I beg of you to let me see him now. He would wish it. He would not forgive you for turning me away now."

"Come, tell me what is the matter and I will help you."

"No, it is you who have done this harm and now he alone can save us."

Simo sent the slaves back to their quarters. Then he turned to her again: "In what way have I harmed you?"

"You do not wish to help us," she said. "The Leno's boat has arrived at the island and my mistress Glycerium and all the household of Chrysis have been sold to him as slaves. We were awakened in the middle of the night by the herald of the village and told to gather our clothes together and to go down to the harbor. Glycerium is not well now; she must not be driven so. I myself escaped through the rows of a vineyard and have come to find Pamphilus. It was you who have done this, for it was the Fathers of the Island who ordered that we should be sold as slaves to pay our debts."

This was true. He remembered having listened without interest to a discussion of the matter, assuming that it would be carried out with sufficient warning and delay to admit of Glycerium's being separated from the rest of the destitute company. The Leno's boat visited Brynos so seldom that it seemed to the Fathers of the Island that they might yet be under the necessity of providing for the house-

hold through many months while await-
ing the arrival of this purchaser.

Suddenly a light dawned upon Mysis:
"He is at the temple! How could I have
forgotten that he was under the vow of
silence and that he must be there!" And
turning she started to enter the road.

"You must not go to him at the
temple," said Simo sharply. "I shall
come down to the harbor with you
now and buy your mistress from the
Leno."

He returned to the house for his cloak,
then walked into the town with Mysis
hurrying at his heels. Dawn was breaking as he descended the winding stairs to
the square. Against the streaked sky he
saw the mast of the Leno's boat. The
Leno was not only a dealer in slaves; he
was a wandering bazaar and sold foreign
foods and trinkets and cloths. If an

island were large enough he came ashore and conducted a fair and a circus. And now in the first cold light of morning Simo could see on the raised portion of the deck a brightly colored booth, a chained bear, an ape, two parrots, and other samples of the Leno's stock in trade, including the household of Chrysis. Philocles had remained on shore and for two hours had been standing at the parapet uttering short broken cries towards his companions. Being a Greek citizen he could not be sold into slavery and was to be transported later to Andros.

Simo descended the steps of the landing with Mysis and was rowed out to the boat. While he concluded his transaction with the black and smiling Leno Mysis sank upon her knees before Glycerium, telling her of this good fortune. But Glycerium derived no joy from the news. She sat between Apraxine and the Ethiopian girl, amid the bundles of their clothes, and for weariness she could scarcely raise her eyes or move her lips. "No," she said, "I shall stay here with you. I do not wish to go anywhere."

Simo approached them. "My child," he said to Glycerium, "you are to come with me now."

"Yes, my beloved," Mysis repeated into her ear, "you must go with him. All will be well. He is taking you ashore to Pamphilus."

Still Glycerium remained with bent head. "I do not wish to move. I do not wish to go anywhere," she said.

"I am the father of Pamphilus. You must come with me and good care will be taken of you."

At last and with great difficulty she arose. Mysis supported her to the side of the boat and there taking her farewell she whispered to her: "Goodbye, my dear love. Now may the gods bring you happiness. I shall never see you again, but I pray you to remember me, for I have loved you well. And wherever we are, let us remember our dear Chrysis."

The two women embraced one another in silence, Glycerium with closed eyes. At last she said: "I would that I were dead, Mysis. I would that I were long dead with Chrysis, my dear sister."

"You are to come with us too," said Simo to Mysis, who having known even greater surprises obediently followed him. The little group was rowed in silence to the shore. The Leno's oarsmen struck the water, his bright colored sails were raised, and his merchandise left the harbor for other fortunes.

The sun had already risen when Pam-

philus returned with swift and happy
steps to his home. There he discovered
Glycerium sleeping peacefully under his
mother's care. There was not a sound
to be heard on the farm, for his mother,
already invested with the dignity of her
new duties as guardian and nurse to the
outcast girl, had ordered a perfect quiet.
Argo was sitting before the gate, her eyes
wide with wonder and pleasure at the
arrival of this new friend. Simo had
gone to the warehouse and when he returned, for all his happiness, he moved
about with lowered eyes, driven by the
constraint in his nature to act as though
nothing had happened.

In the two days that followed, all their
thoughts were centred about the room
where the girl lay and all their hearts were
renewed under the fragile claims that
Glycerium's beauty and shyness made

upon them. Simo seemed, after Pamphilus, to have best understood her reticence and to have been understood by her; a friendship beyond speech had grown up betwen them. This flowering of goodness, however, was not to be put to the trial of routine perseverance, nor to know the alternations of self-reproach and renewed courage; for on the noon of the third day Glycerium's pains began and by sunset both mother and child were dead.

That night after many months of drought it began to rain. Slowly at first and steadily, the rain began to fall over all Greece. Great curtains of rain hung above the plains; in the mountains it fell as snow, and on the sea it printed its countless ephemeral coins upon the water. The greater part of the inhabitants were asleep, but the relief of the long-expected rain entered into the mood of their sleeping minds. It fell upon the urns standing side by side in the shadow, and the wakeful and the sick and the dying heard the first great drops fall upon the roofs above their heads. Pamphilus lay awake, face downward, his chin upon the back of his hand. He heard the first great drops fall upon the roof over his head and he knew that his father and mother, not far from him, heard them too. He had been repeating to himself Chrysis's lesson and adding to it his Glycerium's last faltering words: "Do not be sorry; do not be afraid," and he had been remembering how with the faintest movement of her eyes to one side, she had indicated her child and said: "Wherever we are, we are yours." He had been asking himself in astonishment wherein had lain his joy and his triumph of the few nights before:

how could he have once been so sure of the beauty of existence? And some words of Chrysis returned to him. He recalled how she had touched the hand of a young guest who had returned from an absence, having lost his sister, and how she had said to him in a low voice, so as not to embarrass those others present who had never known a loss: "You were happy with her once; do not doubt that the conviction at the heart of your happiness was as real as the conviction at the heart of your sorrow." Pamphilus knew that out of these fragments he must assemble during the succeeding nights sufficient strength, not only for himself, but for these others,—these others who so bewilderingly now turned to him and whose glances tried to read from his face what news there was from the last resources of courage and hope, to live on, to live by. But in confusion and with flagging courage he repeated: "I praise all living, the bright and the dark."

On the sea the helmsman suffered the downpour, and on the high pastures the shepherd turned and drew his cloak closer about him. In the hills the long-dried stream-beds began to fill again and the noise of water falling from level to level, warring with the stones in the way, filled the gorges. But behind the thick beds of clouds the moon soared radiantly bright, shining upon Italy and its smoking mountains. And in the East the stars shone tranquilly down upon the land that was soon to be called Holy and that even then was preparing its precious burden.